I0572079

Peeling the Apple

Ursula Clare

Illustrated by Gillian Keen

First Published in Australia in 2023
by Gillian Meredith Books

———————————————

Copyright © Ursula Clare 2023

This work is copyright. Apart from any use as permitted under the Copyright Act 1968, no part may be reproduced, copied, scanned, stored in a retrieval system, recorded, or transmitted, in any form, or by any means without the prior written permission of the publisher.

The right of Ursula Clare to be identified as the author of this work has been asserted by her in accordance with the *Copyright Amendment (Moral Rights) Act 2000.*

First printing October 2023
Printed in Australia by Ingram Spark - Lightning Source LLC

Typeset in Calibri and Mantinia CC

Paperback   ISBN: 978-0-6459477-0-0
Hardcover   ISBN: 978-0-6459477-1-7
Ebook   ISBN: 978-0-6459477-2-4

Illustrated by Gillian Keen

Stock photography: dreamstime.com

Book Layout and Cover Design by
Gillian Meredith Art Studio
Goolwa, South Australia

www.gillianmeredith.com

to my family
past, present and to come

Contents

Garden talk — 7

Garden talk — 9

A storeyed landscape — 11

Marking time — 13

Daisies — 15

Dumb was as good as dead - better to utter — 17

You would have thought that, after all this time, she … — 19

Gone fishing — 21

Playing can get you into trouble — 22

and out of it — 23

Hello — 24

Blood lines — 25

Oh … where art thou? — 26

Leaning in — 27

Riverport Song — 29

The colour of forgiveness — 31

Food — 33

In his kiss — 35

This air is not thin — 36

Tai chi mornings — 37

Early as I went walking … — 38

Megavissey — 39

Foot loose — 41

Pennies from heaven — 43

Celebrity gossip — 44

Stanage Edge   47

Why I didn't buy a book at the Greenlights bookshop   48

Why I did buy a book at the Greenlights bookshop   51

On the Cusp   52

Gravitas   **55**

Brunswick winter   57

Tutelage   59

At the Aquacaf   61

May morning at Watercarr   62

Wayfarer   63

Patchwork   65

The artist   67

Counterpoint   **71**

Forked tongue   73

Chord and discord   74

W.B.Yeats meets Karta Pintingka   77

Water bending   78

Calligraphy   **81**

A black and white calligraphy   83

Molten   **89**

Molten   91

Welcome to another year   93

Afterword   **97**

Acknowledgments   **98**

About the Author   **99**

GARDEN TALK

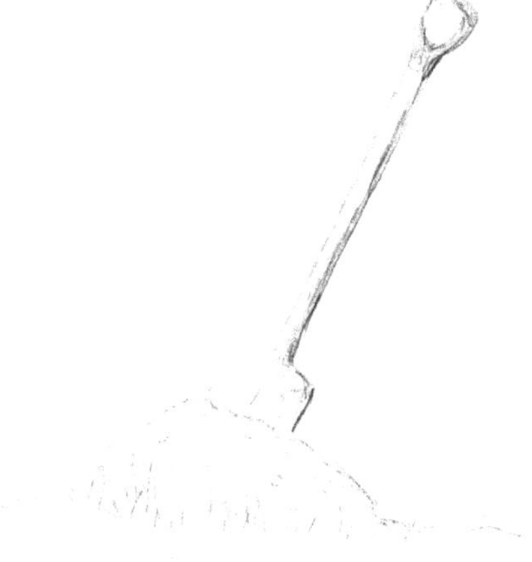

Garden talk

The rain had stopped and we stood
together by the herb patch, making hay
Is your spine a fluid ripple?
My words are a rippling play
She is a potter and likes stretching blocks.

We look down at the dark earth dotted
with self-sown rocket, a wisp of dill
not yet targeted by the plump pigeons
The beetroot are growing well
She reaches for a leaf, hesitates
I am robbing the root.

In my garden rooted tendrils quicken
Bind weed, enough said
Words suck life from the moving finger
You must start in a different place, seek different food
to stoke this sustained endeavour
Those are words, just do it.

I could write a poem about this
I say to my diffidence
The soil under the blue sheet is febrile
crumbling rye grass composted and rich
waiting for its next seed, a mixed crop of
mesclan, the bitter and the sweet.

The words are cool pebbles tossed across the pond
see how that one jumped / a skilful flick
sleight of hand / sleight of mouth / door opens
a tumbling out as though children in galoshes
spill into the garden.
blowing out the windows
exploding in the joy of release

One dill plant grows within a plastic cone protected
The other survives as yet unseen
The greenhouse breathes through an iron lung
its waxen heart swelling and shrinking
out in warmth, in with the cold.

I pick at the dry soil
On the wooden stake a patina of red spider mite
has petrified to sculpture or is it moss?
Who knows what marks are left behind
when the butterfly takes flight.

A storeyed landscape

The lost gardens of Heligan in Cornwall

Four ponds tumbling into each other down the ravine
of feral rhododendrons and exotica brought back
by the botanical adventurers of the nineteenth century.

The first spangled with water lilies, like Chinese blossom
in a porcelain saucer at the bottom of the lawn
sloping down from the squire's house.

The second an oval jewel, fed by hidden fall,
cleared by underwater reed to a translucent surface:
two small islands of reeds and wildflowers rise cleanly
from the sandy bottom.

The third pond is out of sight behind a canopy of palm
and umbrella fronds, northern conifer soaring high into the sky:
just a glistening below the jungle torment.

The fourth pool is yet to be fully dredged, deep in the last valley.

The water flows on to the ram pump in the far field
where it is pushed back up to the reservoir above the house
so it can trickle down again through the vegetable and flower beds
and keep the garden alive.

Marking time

She spent the morning looking at wood.

Dead wood
apricot plum apple peach
the winter harvest.

The orchard is gone now, cleared
by new owners who wanted a shed.

When she takes her knife to the apple twig
it skitters off the crackling bark
before finding purchase
She holds the moment, on outward breath
cuts deep into the last ring of pale clean growth.

Her soft firm hands will sculpt stored life
the play of sunlight
wither of drought
deep drinking

but when she took her blade
to the almond tree on the river bend
she saw it was not time
to cut from trees still living.

...

Walking down to the sea
more than forty years ago
her flaxen haired friend says
You have a pear shaped bottom
Mine is an apple.

Daisies

I went out this morning to pick the flowers
that had opened after the night's sprinkle of rain
soft roll returning after long drought

and I saw that I had a choice
to pick and gather and place in a painted vase
or to leave in place
and paint them into that painted vase
to dip their imaginary stems in imaginary water
to leave the living living
to step away from the dead

and make what I can from these pictures in my eyes
the soft fall, light touch, blush of colour
the trembling edge
all growing in their own perfection
to their own demise.

DUMB WAS AS GOOD AS DEAD - BETTER TO UTTER

Carol Ann Duffy

You would have thought that, after all this time, she ...

The voice hung on the long exhalation searching
but a sudden gust of opprobrium blew words away
before thought could claim the substance of sound.

I was thinking about retail therapy as I sat
in the waiting room in a soft upholstered chair
leafing through the magazines placed tastefully
on the glass chrome table.

For the three folding notes I will surrender
in a mean thank you for an hour's listening to not very much
I could buy that train ticket to Blackpool
return for an extra pound thrown in
or the magnolia bush in a twelve inch pot
with its youth already done
or five days of groceries at Sainsbury's
for I know well how to pare flesh to the bone.

But I am not buying today
I am here to sell my secrets
If I pay will you please take them away
and shake them over the gorse bush
so that their bubbles burst
and the unhappiness caught all those years ago
will float free like the fuzz from exhausted flowers
which have spent their seed.

Bluebells in the bracken
mark the passing of the spring.

Gone fishing

I am not a therapist, the man said.
I sit beside a conversation and I fish
putting a line in here or there, looking
for nooks and crannies away from the main flow
I don't like hooks
I find worms or dragonflies
better bait for the frightened
slimy shapes that glisten when
the light strikes below the surface.

When I sit with my pen
hovering above the page
I think of this fisherman
as I drop my lure into the primordial
bacterial soup of my brain
I wonder what it will catch today.

Down in the depths on the ocean's floor
there are ten thousand life forms, they say,
that have never seen the light.

Playing can get you into trouble

I would
If I could
But I can't
So I shan't
Do what I
Should

I could
If I would
But I shan't
So I can't
Do what I
Should

I could if I would
But I won't so I don't

His glare stoppers my tongue
Shoulders brace to take the weight
Of those slippery insinuating shoulds

First the warning
sh sh sh sh
Then the thud
d d d d

D

and out of it

In the garden see the fairies
tasseled orbs of silk spun seed
lifting, twisting in the sunlight
teasing with the dancing breeze

Dancing children run to catch them
hold them soft in chaliced hands
toss them free and with puffed kisses
send them off to enchanted lands

Hello

Great Owled glasses
Brown rippled hair
atop a wraith of body

Long cardigan hugged
bright blue sticks
A stiff passage

I turned to watch
the tiny mound of buttock
as she slipped away

You are too thin
and I reached out
and met myself
the other in this encounter
fifty years on

and my heart ached
on a surge of ..
a surge of ..
surge of ..
surge

Blood lines

Our daughter left this morning
She slammed the door on an
argument about celery
It's too expensive, I said
It'll reduce your blood pressure
she said

She knows too much about
calories and constituents
and I told her so
Get a life, I said
I'll show you, she said

We didn't hear for six weeks
Worried ourselves sick and I
had to go to the doctor for pills
I didn't try the celery
She's eighteen, the police said

She turned up with
a bunch of poppies
I got a job, she said
Cooking for the Salvos
See you sometime.

Oh ... where art thou?

Try walking
heel to toe and toe to heel
in a straight line

The hound of heaven
bays at the moon
Heel, you slobbering cur

alone alone alone
alone on the wine dark sea
and never a saint took pity
on my soul in agony

Sweet seduction
alone alone alone ...

the moon a soft pillow
upon which to lay a wetted cheek

Out of the words
the communion wafer

the thinnest slice
melting in the touch

Leaning in

leached bone
shrinking muscle
cautious
a hand stretches

might not
even
a feather
brushing past
bruise
if blood lies
too close
to skin
so thin

the boat rocks
in the slight breeze

RIVERPORT SONG

come down to the water, water ...

The colour of forgiveness

We travel to the lake.
Pushing out the old canoe
balancing its flat-bottomed swell
I am suddenly on another lake in another country
listening for the call of the loons
and the flat slap of beaver tail

That canoe is made of fine planked cedar
the paddled water dark with foothills peat
high mountains edge the west

This gentle rocking has taken me there
the roll of sleek red-bellied hull as it rides
the scurry of water whipped by the ocean wind

That canoe is with another man and as if another life
I see the fish slab at the campground smeared with guts
Silver blade slashes silvered skin of pickerel and bass
stripping pearly flesh as though by sleight of hand
I went back in another year alone
to say goodbye to the vanished banished children

Now in the silty waters of real time
I settle to the instability
I know this, I trust this, I like this little canoe.

...

Exploring in a different kind of play
I am told that light is texture, texture light
Black the incontrovertible base
White a dazzle of high frequency
Grey the neutral point

Mortal sin consigns a soul to hell
Innocence smiles from cherub wings
Venal living spots the wafer
until we eat and are made whole

Grey stands between and in equal value
to the all reflective and the non reflective
Grey makes living possible, in the half light

...

The rising sun paints the bed into soft opulence
catching the peaks and troughs of the flung cover
a rumple of summer blue in the edging of the sheets
Propped pillows hold the imprint of my entrance to this day

No grey to be seen
but it is there there   there
in all passage, in each modulation of shifting tone.

Food

I took Regret out to lunch today
She'd dropped by yesterday
while I was clearing boxes
and looped an arm across my shoulder

I stiffened for prepared rebuke
but did not shrug
letting it lie, this claim, this chain,
and went about my business

Today she surprised me with a friendly face
so I took her down to the beach cafe
to celebrate my return
Mulloway with salsa, a local white
coffee framed by chocolate
sweet cousin to that long memory
of a margarita's salty kiss

...

That Sunday bloomed in the warm fresh air
down at the river mouth, pelicans in flotilla,
stick humans on the far shore mimicking the scatter
of black waders on the sandbar, content to co-exist
I pranced around the tide soaked headland
samphire offering springy passage
across the grey sucking mud
On Monday I sank into a creamy bog
milk and bananas, dense rye bread.

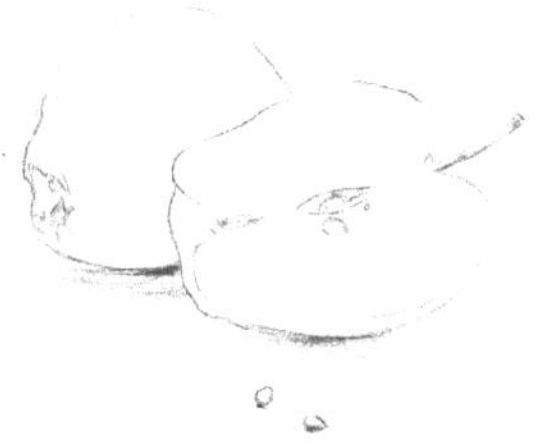

In his kiss

She went down to the jetty for daybreak's song
Rounding the corner on the homeward run
She met a man carrying orange sarong.

She was headed for tea and book
Come with me, he said as he swung
Black bathers, dangling as his hook.

In her hand the emptied mug was begging
For that first caffeine slug to fuel a day
Of words to be written: she feared reneging
On purpose and the righteous way
But the sway of this man she will not ignore
And she turned, as she had turned before.

At river's edge they laughed aloud
At the sign that said swimming not allowed
And climbed down to the water unbowed.

Launching into shimmer of golden light
Bracing the cold left by the night
Shivering as they dried and trundled back
To shower and breakfast and the morning's chat
Of youthful love and young despair
And being on the edge of what is there.

This air is not thin

Captain Charles Sturt, diary entry,
Goolwa Channel, 12 February 1830:

> *To our right the thunder of the heavy surf, that almost shook*
> *the ground beneath us, broke with increasing roar upon our*
> *ears; to our left the voice of the natives echoed through the*
> *bush*

You can hear the children calling
as they dash around the playground
scrambling up the rigging
splashing at water's edge
Up on the crest above the elbow of the river
around the old meeting place the bushland whispers
Jekejere, Jekejere, as the cars whoosh past.

Bastions of settlement line descent to the water
a five minute stroll through two hundred years
sand-stoned justice now a cultural hub
In the prison laundry noted for its triplet tub
an artist covers canvas with the passage of her time.

She draws on country that has drawn her
as holiday child, as honeymoon bride,
brought her down to the river to settle and paint
the glancing dancing light of each returning day.

She tells of a morning when the wind roared in
sudden through the open door, lifting the matting
into dusty dragon, flaked paint swirling, her studio
twirling in elemental cavort and she in the middle
with her brush painting its trace. In a high corner
dry-fronded stalks clump casually in a tin pail.
Jekejere. Ngurunderi. Reed song.

Signal Point Gallery, Goolwa, February 2018
Ground floor: *Jacob Stengel, Karumapuli - My Country*
Upstairs: *Threads of Thought, The Language of Stitch: an exhibition of*
the work of 36 textile artists

Tai chi mornings

fair lady weaves the shuttle
rabbit digs the earth
needle on the seabed

The yellow bobbles float in a linked chain from the reedy shoreline,
where the heron stands, to the break in the barrage, entrance to the lock.
From the far shore a matching yellow chain echoes the scalloped curve,
a protective claim, channelling passage to the sea.
Here the river becomes estuary, ocean meets drainage from the land.

The yellow cuts vividly across the grey water, breaking the lines of the ripples.
It cannot be unseen. The instructional iPod cannot be unheard.
The marshalling words, against a tinkle of instrumented sound, beat loudly
 into the music of the water and the birds and the rustle of the wind.
 Attend, attend: both eye and ear are summoned.

One bobble in the chain, a paragraph of text,
a loop in the thread, such timeworn practice
this telling of the beads as they slip through our fingers.

Early as I went walking ...

I'd woken to a strong beat
and went out to pound heat
into the grey morning
I'd seen the sun dawning
red across eastern sky
I'd heard the black birds cry.

Two figures ahead so I skirted
wide around the corner and
emboldened by distance spoke
of the orange beanie on the head
of the matchstick girl
but look, your feet are bare
just a stripe of blue thong.

The river ahead lures me
to boast of swimming rubber clad
no care for hands or feet
but oh the pain of open face
Yesterday, the girl says,
I went into the sea with my black cap
and winter wetsuit and it was fine
until I met a seal and scampered
back, fearing attack. Yes.
How to know friend from foe.

I too went barefoot, said the other,
bare-headed bundled mother
Now I keep my feet warm.

We've wrapped the moment.
I increase my pace.

Megavissey

During the night the seagulls call across the boats
anchored in the tidal swell of the fishing bay
A croaking cry, a drawn out call like the splash of
black ink across parchment, sudden, full and tapering
a pattern caught and repeated, shorter, slower,
diminuendo, and then nothing until I tune again
to the patter of rain, the sough of the sea wind.

FOOT LOOSE

Pennies from heaven

I was surprised by the white sliver of lightning
how thin it was, a mean line
not much grace flowing from the divine source
to pierce those remnants of suffering humanity
cowering amid the dark mass of
rock   air   water

My words are as lurid as those painted giants,
nineteenth century melodrama hung on the millennium
She likes the detail better
the fine weave on Canute's sleeve as he sits
on tide-embroidered shore and
commands the sea to stand still

This artist turned engineer
drew beautiful plans that cost him all
His sewage work could have saved a million lives

The entrance sign mocks
The end is nigh, donate now
Art foretells its own apocalypse

Outside a mother bustles past
one child tucked
the other, freely frolicking
around the stands of tea-towelled art,
wants to feed the steel-sprung monster.
I've spent all my pennies, she says
Where, he asks, precise.
On the bus.

The soft whoosh of Yorkshire vowel
grounds all pretension.

*John Martin: Painting the Apocalypse
at the Millennium Gallery in Sheffield*

Celebrity gossip

Ms Alexandra Debrett is honeymooning
with Joshua Smith, her third husband,
on his yacht in Sicily.

Alexandra, a soft girl, must have got it from her dad,
that hopeful eye. Not that I blamed him.

Her mum, the Honourable Mrs, was a piece of work.
I knew her type, grew up with them on Messina streets,
those girls who primped and pranced their way
into silken sheets and champagne breakfasts,
touting what they had of nature's gifts,
a fine brow, soft sculptured cheek,
the bloom of youth, that questing lift of lip.

Oh yes, I knew her.
My sister was one such.
She made it to America
on a banker's purse,
didn't write home again.
Does she too now eat
prunes in bed for breakfast
before she hides her wrinkles
under the day's painted mask?

Maid to the family, twenty years ago, hired to
clean and cook, I sussed soon the entrails
of that marriage. I've skinned and gutted enough
rabbits in my time to know what's what.
The man was trapped. Bored, she'd let him play,
come home late until, smelling danger
to title, to rite of place, she'd pounce.

From my bedroom alcove in the kitchen
I heard the screeching in the hall,
the air ablaze, daughters mewing.

With what glee do I now remember
how I set their dough to prove
in the foetid hollow of my rumpled bed.

Stanage Edge

We live in a poisoned dome, the youngish man said,
coming north for Easter, down to the country
where the real people live.

They sprinkle the moorlands, still browned
by last year's wintered growth,
with burble from the films and music of their youth;
three generations of this familial tribe
climbing slowly between the granite boulders
that have tumbled from the high edge
and the hand-worked wheels of stone
strewn in testimony to some abandoning fate.

They picnic by the hanging rock.
Come under the shadow of this red rock
says the older man to the older woman.
She averts her gaze, shy in the sharing
of another heritage, uncertain of the ground.
The party splits. He turns back, she walks on.

She finds the words where she thought she would,
in Eliot's Waste Land, the burial of the dead.

Why I didn't buy a book at the Greenlights bookshop

on 686 Fulton St, Fort Greene, Brooklyn, New York

I am travelling light
there is no room
for more weight
no room in my pack
no room in my head

Like fire-flies the words
on the turning page
spark and dim
as my eyes speed
a million words
a million pages
converging
in this book store
at this moment
on October 8, 2016

I didn't buy a book
I want slow words
not this insistent beat, the pavement pounded
the promise, the drive, the wonder
of it all, the charge, oh if only, if only
I was I could I did ...

Enough that I take the moment
of not buying a book
on trust, in faith, not
a moment to be snared
on the wing, pinned, packed

and I go back to my air b n b
dark in the humid day as the engines throat around
that moment, this moment, type type type
plucking words from the froth and bubble

The dog writes on the window with his nose …
I rub my eye along the page
my breath rising

I am not buying
Yet …

Why I did buy a book at the Greenlights bookshop

on 686 Fulton St, Fort Greene, Brooklyn, New York

Patti Smith lies waiting
Our granddaughter has lent her bed
and offers me the book beside
because I lent her Patti's first, Just Kids,
her ex-boyfriend has it should she go and
claim it no no I say I just need
to know where it is in its travels
and I cannot take your M Train
because it's hard backed and it's yours.

When we meet on our last morning
backpacked, ready for the bus to Boston
we walk to the studio where she starts
the week's practice, she's a dancer
spreading her life away from home, away, away
and after we look at the old synagogue
and the meeting room with the stained glass
in which lie bodies stretching in leg warmers
we continue up Fulton Street
to the Greenlights Bookstore.

I have found a crumb.
Of course they have it
although I ask for My Train.

The dog writes on the window with his nose …

On the Cusp

Sunday August 31, 2014

On the cusp
the wind blowing from the north west
balmy still in the sunshine, the azure sea
of the early sky studded now with billowing cloud
We talk transitions under the lime tree
I spout words: mess, let go,
cannot know if you continue to hold

The boy clinging to his mother's leg
will not let go of the supporting hand, hesitates
to take that first unaided step, feet unshod
Will he too learn that it's the space between one step
and the next that holds the promise

The season swings towards the autumnal equinox
We will meet its vernal counterpart as we head south
the sun in balance, perpendicular to both hemispheres
We will come back at the solstice
summer to winter, from light to dark
I rest before I spring

Wednesday August 30, 2017

On the iPhone
the boy says to the man
who has stopped by a verge on the underside of the world
to say hallo before a long drive home
make sure you take enough gravity in the car
Grandpa

GRAVITAS

Brunswick winter

I did not know that you were gone.
As the frog in slowly heating water feels not the advent of its death
so I in mounting absence of your sound, your fleshy move,
noted not the slackening muscle, cerebellum's crisp,
until aboard the tram these shuffling, stuttering, splattering bodies
doing their awkward dances, telling their clattering tales,
spilled across my canvas like fresh blooded paint.

Ah, the shock of it.
I have become ghost, hostage to the word.
Winter's burnt my stored wood, laid wet char to source my ink.
Like fringe of blackened eucalypt by fire-swept country road
I am stripped to hieroglyph, a cypher shrunk to fit the page.

In footage at the gallery
the painter, rising beast-like from the lake,
lifts a pelican from the wild shore
and flings its withered carcass again and again
against paper laid across the uncleared ground,
grinding, screwing, forcing passage from this body in decay
to another form of life, a seminal exchange.

On the tram again, secure upon my seat,
I'm tracing bodies with my eyes, the fall and tuck of fabric
cling to belly, flounce of faded cotton, suited edge,
the droop of day's commute. And then above the rattle
a trill, a feathered tickling in my ear, a thread of song
as soft and light as dust motes catching rays of sun.

A woman stands at carriage end, black tights in sturdy boots,
and yellow cut-offs, purple top, a gleaming helmet of black hair.
Beside a man sits drab and still, but see now, there's
a flutter in his cheek, the faintest dimpled pulse, no quiver
on his lips, but he's the instrument, if not the source.

Gleeful in conspiracy we share a fleeting smile
this girl (she's still a girl) and I for a moment linked
in magic triangle, an unspoken trinity.
The tram stops. We go our separate ways.

When winter lifts and the ti-tree flowers
I place that moment on this page,
as signal of your sweet return.

Tutelage

For Jean in Canada

Will the snow be gone before we say goodbye?
Last night long winter froze the pushing thaw
and whitened yet again the bludgeoned earth
as if to taunt such faith in growth renewed
and I who visit now from southern warmth
must learn again a patience for those ways
in which confinement may enrich the day
and constraint is no bar to being free.

We stand, my friend and I, at kitchen sink
to look through slatted blind and tripled glass
on backyard clutter turned to sun-etched art
of shadow fold and crystal shine and blue
A fleeting view which offers fitting frame
to treasure stored within these time worn walls.

Expect no silverware nor golden trim
no grand design, no claim to high estate
This simple house exhales munificence
more subtly expressed: a fragrant air
of love and loss distilled throughout the years;
the echoed beat of footfall through the rooms
in practised measure of each valued day
that's shared with hope upheld and heartfelt care.

There's flint from Scottish forebears in these bones
a forceful will that gives no sentiment
to cloying grief for what there cannot be
Her home is clear and open to the light
It is a gallery where pictures hang
to celebrate anew the world's romance.

This artist, though she does disclaim the name,
takes emptied form and builds with prescient eye
and penciled stroke on stroke such sculptured light
and colour on the page that eyes must touch
They took us in, my infant child and I,
to layer her youth with ribbons of delight
and melodies of gritty tender love
that have held us close these thirty years and more.

And now we stand, my friend and I, by sink
where once she washed my daughter's feet, as hip
to hip we read aloud my garden talk
of spider mite and winter's covered growth
I leave her at the window, sitting straight
She's reading "Lark Rise" and I hear her song.

At the Aquacaf

His words dropped like a hook into the lace of the conversation,
this meeting of old friends bearing witness.

That absence and my eyes stopped hearing the surround
and my eyes saw the hole in the fabric stretching
a fossil of air, entrance to a labyrinth of unforgetting.

This absence has been a gift he said of his parents'
retreat from expectation, their barricaded hearts.
He extends his left forearm, draws back the cloth,
exposes the imprinted words: *tabula rasa*
I was given an empty canvas upon which to paint my life.
The page waits, full of what has not been said.

Three months after his father's death, no tears shed,
the son frets that he may not have had a good dying.
Across the rigid face of the old man lying
he'd seen an anxious shift, a sudden lift
as though in startle at an escaping fear.
His father died alone that night
without the comfort he had not sought,
never offered to his son. Who now dreads
what may lie beneath filial duty,
his encompass of the widowed man.
We were all around when my mother died,
he said. She had a good death.

That fossil of breath, the widening hole,
the proffered arm. Out from the ghosts
of lest we forget stretch all those tattooed
numbers on all that tender skin.

May morning at Watercarr

breakfast in the sunshine
in the sheltered nook
outside the kitchen window
feet bare on the warming stone

and the sun's low rays
touched the forget-me-nots
growing wild on the gravelled path
and the green fronds and the blue flowers
cast shadow dark across flat grey stone
dark in the curve of inner arch
opening over the brace of bone
and there the shadow stopped
and there it lay smiling
my tattoo of forget-me-nots
warmed to sepia by the run
of blood beneath the skin.

Wayfarer

Early one morning in the city of Pisa
leaving sisters asleep in the Borgo Suite
I walked along the Arno to the old city wall
where Galileo stands by St Agnes's tower
hands poised to invoke, fingers crooked.
Around the corner I came upon a green sward
and white butterflies cavorting in the sunshine
and a sprinkle of yellow daisies dotted with
the occasional button of blue. I danced there
by the river in wonder at the world's
celebration of my seventy five years.

People passed as I practised. Five women
red capped on the water rowing under loose
command, no chiding of the dangling oar
as they rounded their skiff downstream.
A young woman cycling across the bridge
turned her head to watch me
and returned my silent salute.

I plucked a frond before I left
two blue flowers on a straggling stem
woven into birthday buttonhole.
My sisters greeted me with candled peach,
a rosy mound edged with plum,
Caravaggio on a small white plate.
I added my fading flowers, a little sad.
Then on screen sent to honour this day
a perfect spangle of blue floret, radiant.
My blue eye of a flower. *Wegwarte*
my sister said. It grows along the pathways.
It's a watcher of the way.

I looked it up when I came home
exchanging Italian saunter through sun-struck stone
for dark-wrapped bodies leaning into Yorkshire chill.
It's the flower of chicory from the daisy family
no one knows for sure from where the name

for the bitter root with its rose blushed leaves
and the bright blue flowers that wilt on picking.
A healing herb widely known
from the beginning of recorded time.
Wayfarer   watching   waiting

Patchwork

returning to arrive again
at the edge of the sea

arriving to return again
to the edge of the sea

not … not yet … not yet back …
there is no turning back

Out of the fog of awakening
the tree so clear in the clear dawn
is a puzzle, to the left all spiky filigree
on the right dark broad-brushed crags
arching … arcing …
and the uniting trunk of the tree resolves
into frame of the mirror's separate panes.

Out of brain fog a hot air balloon lifts

as though out of Corot's painted mists
or the wheat fields of the Wimmera, softly green
and golden in the rain-pearled sunlight
or the cottonwool of forgetting blanketing
the tree tops of the wet flatland farms
that stretch from Amsterdam to Copenhagen

suspended, waiting for the wind

a patchwork balloon, lifted
from a true story of a family
creative in escape
who sew the fabric of their lives
into a balloon of many colours
and float from east to west
over the high barbed wire
above sentries primed to kill.

Down on the ocean beach
the howl of the gale from the west
faced full frontal
entered my ear whorls
mounted to dervish scream.
Turning cheek left and right
I marvelled at the calm
then continued along the edge
where the skimming water
settled the whipping sand.

The artist

She was sitting in the corridor
on guard beside an open door
upright on a wooden chair
a dark bundle of bone
with a shock of white hair

Hello Ann, we said brightly
and she lifted her black eyes
to look first at the one of us
and then at the other
and back to the one
who was saying remember
and back to the other

then she reached forward
to paint with her finger
a downward curve of
shadow on my left cheek
and an upward stroke of
light on the right

a smudge of purple
and a whinge of green
It's good to see you

We walked with her to her big white room
We helped her on to her high white bed
The walls are bare
otherwise they bother her

You can go now

She has gone now

We'll scatter her grit on the gorse-flamed heath
above a simple stone cottage on the green Dorset coast.
In a small white bedroom her painting hangs
of shadow on a white barn wall
beside a countering slab of mudded stone
and my eyes are blocked wide, held to ransom

until I must stop and attend with respect
to the challenge of those marshalling planes
before I slip between the two buildings
and follow the track past the sun-bleached clothes
flapping on a line stretched between the olive trees
and note in the distance her streak of cobalt sea
edging the powder blue of that Ionian sky.

COUNTERPOINT

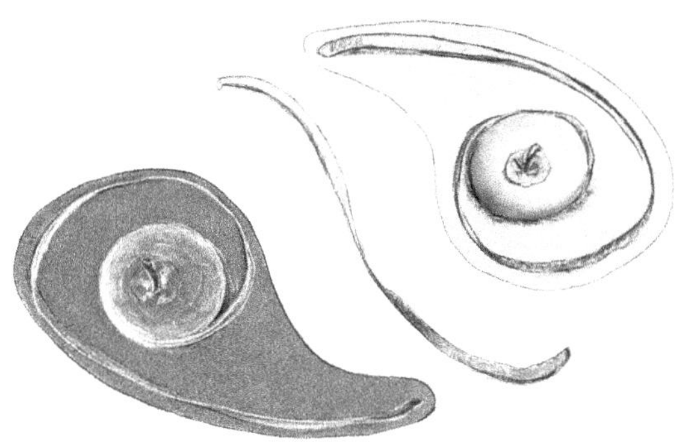

Forked tongue

She stirred the embers of the campfire
rehearsing to the new arrival
the returning immigrant
the words she'd heard rising
from the land of her birth
which is not the land of her language

listening to the survivors
who are not going away

and as she stirs
she is smudged by her telling
of that dark release
and a white curl lifts
from the ashes that cover
the wood of all those words
burning bright in the heart of things

Chord and discord

I hear the blackbird in the magpie's song
as the round moon sinks in the western sky
and to the east from whence the bird sings
no blush of dawn.

It sang so sweet that I ask
indeed what bird is this
from what clime. It is no matter.
The bird sings sweetly with
repeated refrain, exploring
variation in a rising trill
writing its notes on the sea's low roar.

...

Come for a walk, she says to my importuning.
Ah, a kinaesthetic unease
not a sour and sorry potage.

You can love a man who is not a feminist.

What have we done to make us think
we are so entitled. Sex is not
a commodity which you can take to
the check-out counter and then decide
not to buy, put back on the shelf.

If you swim in the pools above the waterfall
risking the river's flow you might
get swept over in unpredicted surge.

We are not computer simulations
turned off with a click. Chemistry
explodes. We are not just text.

...

A metaphor can be trinket
jewelled necklace
a line of blood from the beheading
a garrotte at the throat.
Women knitted as
the tumbrils brought those necks
to be sliced by the knife.

Under the metaphor, the dust and the clay

...

In the marketplace in Katmandu
the pots are laid in serried ranks
platooned across the square.
As the sun heats a woman
indeed a girl moves
between each line turning
the pots one at a time
to move each cheek to face the sun
so the drying is gentle and even,
does not stress, will not fracture.

In the stalls the beans and grains settle in their sacks
Baskets of spice and herb mound.
Brown arm offers a cascade of beads and silver
a waterfall of threaded drop,
threaded clay, threaded light.
Bartering with cold cash, we have
full stomachs, empty hearts.

After the earthquake, dust and clay

...

the sun hits my mirror in a full peel of light
out of the grey cloud hanging over the coast.
It silvers as I write, has had its moment,
leaves pink blush on my retina
as it returns to monochrome print,
an etching. I have been blinded.
Bow your heads
Do not stare at these gods.

...

Shall I cut my jib to suit your cloth?
Better to have lived and lost?

W.B.Yeats meets Karta Pintingka

Kangaroo Island, South Australia

It could be Aegean, this gold and turquoise sea
The land is dry enough, bleached and greyly writhing
those tree trunks, not statured olives gnarled with age,
these are wispy, tall, singing to a rougher wind
with the rocks breaking sharp over sharks teeth
black in the creaming foam.

We made ourselves a nest
back from the cliff's edge
in a clump of sloping casuarinas
and watched two eagles circling
in the swirl of lifting air
as though in play until one drops
down down straight as a stone
into a dark tangled creature
tossed up on the bedrock

and I, reared on Mediterranean myth,
see swan tearing into maiden flesh.
I cannot name the local Zeus
who chased his two escaping wives
and conjured up a storm to sweep them
from the rocks and they drowned
and rose as the two black crags
in the sea beyond the sunset edge
of this island of the dead.

Seal encrusted, foul mouthed whalers
raided mainland and brought back their blood
tossed like that wrack of sea grass
flotsam … and on the story goes …

Ovid did not call it rape.

Words impregnate the experience
turning inward to the texture
outward to a narrative
opening to embrace the taloned claw,
the surging thrust, the surrender.

Water bending

Limpet
clinging to the rock
mollusc with a muscular foot
holds tight as the waves crash
swim it hears the mermaid cry
but it will not be torn away
matching fight to might
force against flow

let the wave desist
water soften wind slow
and in the gentle massage
of the quiet stillness
tentacles relax
that frantic sucking grip
and open to the invitation

Liminal
that space between
dreaming and waking
night and day
dark and light

Limpid
transparent, translucent no longer
these lens with which I was born
cataract, waterfall, floodgate
too much seeing, too much light
battering the eye's defence
my sight dims and blurs

I hope I get a silicone replacement.
I like that it comes from sand.
Acrylic is a petroleum product
and has more to answer for.

When the dark arrives that evening ... and Andrew goes for pizza, horrid but I didn't have to cook, I'm cooking for my birthday ... he calls me out to look at the star in the western sky ... a planet ... he sees its light streaming out in three or four directions. I see that too, see more than three ... and when I take off my glasses it explodes like a Christmas sparkler, a star burst. See the moon, he says, turning to the east, it's several days off full ...

and the mounding disc of reflected light shines silver in a sea of deep royal blue, a rich wide ring of blue around a silver pupil - ring, ring, the bell rings - segueing out in thinning circles through the whole spectrum, from green to yellow through all the colours in between to a rim of rusty red, before night reclaims the sky.

He only sees the moon. Will I only see the moon?

CALLIGRAPHY

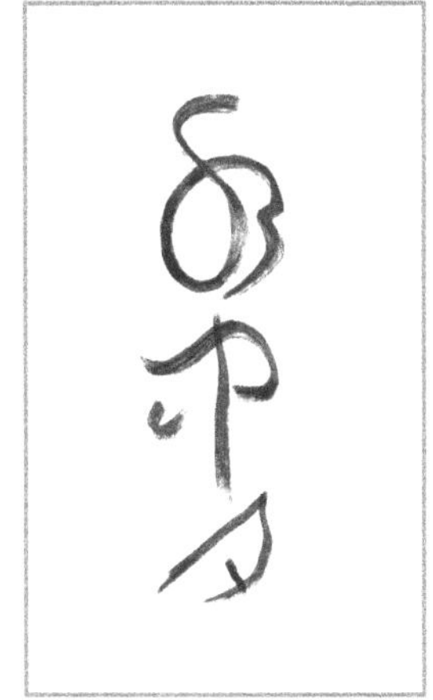

A black and white calligraphy

I

St. Peter was waiting for me at the gate.
He'd seen my approach and came unshaven.
Keys into lock, he directs my eyes
to the seal on the bank.
They know to shelter, he says.

He opens the gate and we stand
within on the iron foot bridge
and watch the seals duck and roll,
the gannets and the cormorants
the divers and the pelicans.
Are there many? More than forty
at the mouth. I'd take a howitzer
to them but the pollies won't act
too much outcry about baby faces
the survival of the fittest
just wait until they threaten us
and not just a few fisherman
not just the native life that
we've been so good at killing off.

Black, the seals, the birds, the beard.

Later, with the wind rising, I return alone
to cross to the lock, the river upstream
rumpled and restless, to the east
under the lee of concrete slab still
as a salty millpond, cordoned.

Ahead a diver flaps and flutters
on the fretted iron, lifting only to fall again.
It rests as I stop and wait
and when I start again, it tries
again and fails again to rise above
the caging sides of the bridge.

Peeling the Apple

I turn my eyes to the water and
as though released from their grasp
only as I turn back to passage
do I catch feet scrabbling on the railing
wings opening, steadying
and I see the bird fly out and down
see it wheel and rise and I
laugh and clap and cheer
its escape, the mended wing,
its black calligraphy.

II

The wind is strong and cold and gusting,
rain threatens, we do our tai chi
in the gazebo, the shelter … St.Peter thought of heaters
a hearth for the fire … dancing around the fire …
I'm pulled into the inner circle, close my eyes
to shield my brain, I cannot be so still, not yet.

I have an affection for that place in the corner
by the opening, looking across to the barrage,
one eye turned outwards as the words and
the music boom, feeding the space

and as I sank and lifted, rose and fell
in the instructed rhythm of my breath
I felt that feather I'd seen drifting
down from verandah edge
to ground after the storm

and I saw how a feather might fall
in the same move to earth as
a ton of bricks, a virgin's tomb,
a stack of books, a library
if it were to fall in perfect stillness
at the still point, where the dance is
and all I was doing was to breathe in and out
into the stillness and see how soft
and how precise and how strong
each little fuzz of feather was

and how ink ran down from the quill
dipped into ground pigment, running
across the page and how
gentle was inexorably
the art of the sword.

III

The slope to water's edge is a muddy slime
with tufts of grass to anchor feet.
Words ripple up as the water ripples in
floating light as that feather
constructed in the breath
sink and lift, rise and fall
listening to the words emerging
soft as spider silk from the surround.

IV

On the jetty plum in the middle
on the cross piece
stood a long-beaked, snake-
necked, web-footed diving bird.
Its downy breast and the spiky
disorder of wing, the tortoiseshell fringe
on the forking tail still hazed by fluff
told me this bird was young
as it stood there, twisting, craning
left and right in a serpentine display.

I went for camera to catch
the beauty of that new laid pattern
the embroidery on the wings.

On return I thought it gone
but no, it had moved to the corner
pink-webbed claws steady on the stanchion
allowing me room to dance.
From the corner of my eye I saw
the bird settle, fluff out its breast
tail feathers become porcupine quills

a spit of dusty pink at throat
as though collar to match
those big big fleshy feet.

I left it at perch, came back for my porridge.

V

I woke at my birthing hour
with a whirring in my head
like feathered wings
a rustling and a flapping
swooping and diving
all those words of the
day's conversations
rippling on in my bed.

Life is beautiful
We won, we won …
So sang the boy
amid the carnage

and I lie not in the dark
because I've turned on the light
and I'm writing as though pulling
words down upon the page
will fend away the feather and
the wings and the snaking heads
with their hidden teeth
that tear at flesh beneath the skin
The wind is howling
the earth is heating up
I need a smoulder to
germinate the seeds
I shut out my dreams of war
I'll know soon enough
of another conflagration.

VI

He says he is a dancer
following music to its source
She says she is a rock
rising from the stream

She says she is a sculptor
edging knife along the grain
He says he is a potter
pressing thumbprint into clay.

MOLTEN

Molten

I

In a British museum full of trophy
the horses prance across the walls
line after line of Trojan steed
huge slabs of heaving marble
rippling flanks and rearing nostrils
trampling hooves and hand held bridles
stilled into a river of stone.

I lifted hand to pat ...
this one here with the charging eye
and felt him quiver and watched
his head come around to nuzzle for
for the apple that I always bring
on these crisp mornings
before we set out to ride.

II

Those Greeks folded stone
to drape limbs in soft caress
of women stilled in motion
The garb dances ever young.

Ever young that rippled swatch of blue
tied by my mother around my throat
as though to blunt the severing blade
and keep warm those corded sinews
standing guardian to my stricken heart
as we shuffle around goodbye.

III

Waterfall words
those clear light tones
from my daughter's day far away
floating in on the air waves
like crystal melting
green green green
on the morning grass

to rise again gasping
tears of woe spilling
into the sunshine warming
those echoing flutes
of standing stone
as they joined in the song.

IV

Cleft and cleave
Warp and weave
Grapple and grieve
Love and leave.

Welcome to another year

What will get me out of bed
what will help to clear my head
oh my tum is just so sore
I can't cope with any more
in this world of this and that
yes and no compete in spat
this is such a silly rhyme
will I know when it is time

let the fingers dance the tune
as I circle round the room
Hurtle stands upon the chest
must I really now get dressed
keep the rhythm keep the rhyme
slowing down is not a crime
There are many things to love
on the roof stands one white dove

tip tap tip tap on we go
through the wind but not the snow
that softly blankets far up north
and melts to show its passing worth
onward upward round and round
to the march of feet where bound
to the fall of breath we hold
listen listen as we're told

of what's been and what's to come
in the beat and rush and thrum
pigeon feet type on the tin
from afar the ocean's din
waves roll out upon the beach
wash the sands beyond our reach
scrabble scratching go the feet
coo coo coo for softer beat
and so the play goes on and on
and on and on and on and … on

*Hurtle, a little blue papier-mâché elephant, plays a lead role in Fandango with
Elephant, a book I wrote for my granddaughter's first birthday.*

Afterword

on making and being made

Walking and sitting and circling: returning to arrive again, arriving to return.

The experience most readily to mind is a four day walk I did - with my Englishman and his English nineteen year old granddaughter - around the Three Capes stretching into the southern ocean south east of Hobart. Previously only accessible to those fit enough to carry full camping load, there is now an open well-cleared trail, boardwalk laid across under-storey, thicket cleared, stones stepped, useful railing. With stylish bunk room accommodation and spacious kitchens and community space along the way, we needed to carry only bedding and food. A varied terrain, some cliff edge challenge. Every so often along the path, unpredictably, we'd come across a work of art - a mosaic in the rock, sculptured iron or stone, abstracted, a finely crafted useful bench.

I asked the nineteen year old to take a photograph of the spider silk I saw drifting in the wind from the top of a tall tree. She took the photo, but the lens did not capture and pin to the page those slivery flying filaments sketched across the blue. Neither, in her shock, did she film the snake that lay across her path, a blackened stick until it moved slowly away from the tremor of her footfall. Her first snake. She'll have it stored, waiting.

Stored. Storied. My English landscapes are so differently storeyed. In England the roads in early summer are ribboned with red poppies thriving in the untilled verges, watered by run-off from asphalt or the trodden path. They speckle the sown pasture too, companion to blue cornflower and white daisy frond.

Acknowledgments

The poems in this collection arrived because they escaped my constricting fear, released by the kind and honest attention of my writing companions over the last fifteen years. They made it safe to share. I thank Lis Cashdan in England, members of Sandwriters in Goolwa, and most particularly Judy Baghurst, Helen Ellemor, Liz Hobbs, Virginia Lund and Jenni Worth, who have hung in with me through the struggle and the shadows. I thank Patricia Rose and Sally Fox, who first befriended my incipient creativity. I thank Raewyn Morrison and Sherrill Wright for their healing hands. I thank Heather England for the proof-reading. I thank Lesley Parkin and Charlie Denning for being the best neighbours and Lesley particularly for the dance.

It's been a delight to collaborate with Gillian Keen in the making of this book. Her technical and design skills and her artistic talent, together with her 'can do' practicality and her deep compassion make her a reassuringly resourceful and creative partner in our **Never Too Late** enterprise.

Thank you Louise for the resilient friendship.
Thank you Andrew for continuing to listen, surprise and delight.
Thank you Simone for your generous embrace.

About the Author

Ursula Clare was born in Australia to an English mother and German father, who emigrated just before the fracture of yet another war. After a BA in history from Melbourne University, she studied Psychology in London and started her career within the community social and health sector in the UK followed by a decade in northern Canada. She returned to Australia in the 1980's with her young daughter, resolved to settle, only to fall in love with an English cousin and be caught up again in the patterns of hemispherical swing. She now divides her year between Goolwa in South Australia where the River Murray meets the Southern Ocean, and Sheffield in a Yorkshire valley rising up to the moors.

www.ingramcontent.com/pod-product-compliance
Lightning Source LLC
Chambersburg PA
CBHW061127100726
47911CB00013B/709